Time for bed, Isobel

David Bedford & Leonie Worthington

LITTLE HARE

"Time for bed, Isobel," said Mum.

"I don't want to go to bed,"
said Isobel. "I want to be with you."

"You will be with me," said Mum. "I'll be here, doing my exercises."

Isobel crumpled up her bedclothes until they were *just right*, and settled down to sleep.
But after a while...

"I'll do *my* exercises," said Isobel. And she did.
"Well done," said Mum. "You can do them
again tomorrow, if you like.
Now it's time for bed."

"I don't want to go to bed," said Isobel.
"I want to be with you."

"You will be with me," said Mum. "I'll be here,
tidying away your things."

Isobel fluffed up her pillow until it was just right,
and settled down to sleep.
But after a while...

"I'll tidy away my things too," said Isobel.
And she did.

"Well done," said Mum. "You can help me again tomorrow, if you like. Now it's time for bed."

"I don't want to go to bed," said Isobel.
"I want to be with you."

"You will be with me," said Mum.
"I'll be here, reading my book."

Isobel snuggled under her blankets until they were
just right, and settled down to sleep.
But after a while...

"I'll read *my* book," said Isobel.
And she did.

"Well done," said Mum. "We can read some more tomorrow, if you like. Now it's *really* time for bed, Isobel."

Isobel's mum gave her a goodnight kiss,
and Isobel settled down to sleep.
"I don't want to go to bed," whispered Isobel.
"I want to be with you."

"You will be with me," said Mum, yawning.
"I'll be right here, lying next to you."
But after a while...

Mum started to doze.

Mum started to snore.

Mum started to stretch across the bed.

"Wake up, Mum!" said Isobel. "I want to go
to sleep now, but there's no room!"

"Oh dear," said Mum. "Your
bed is so warm and snug I just
couldn't stay awake."

She got up and tucked Isobel in just right.
And after a while...

Isobel went to sleep.

For the wonderful and talented Isobel
—DB

For Hugh, Jack and Phoebe
—LW

Little Hare Books
4/21 Mary Street, Surry Hills
NSW 2010 AUSTRALIA

www.littleharebooks.com

Copyright © text David Bedford 2006
Copyright © illustrations Leonie Worthington 2006

First published in 2006

National Library of Australia
Cataloguing-in-Publication entry

Bedford, David, 1969- .
Time for bed, Isobel.

For children.
ISBN 1 921049 35 9.

1. Bedtime - Juvenile fiction. I. Worthington, Leonie,
1956- . II. Title.

823.92

Designed by Serious Business
Produced by Phoenix Offset, Hong Kong
Printed in China

10 9 8 7 6 5 4 3 2 1